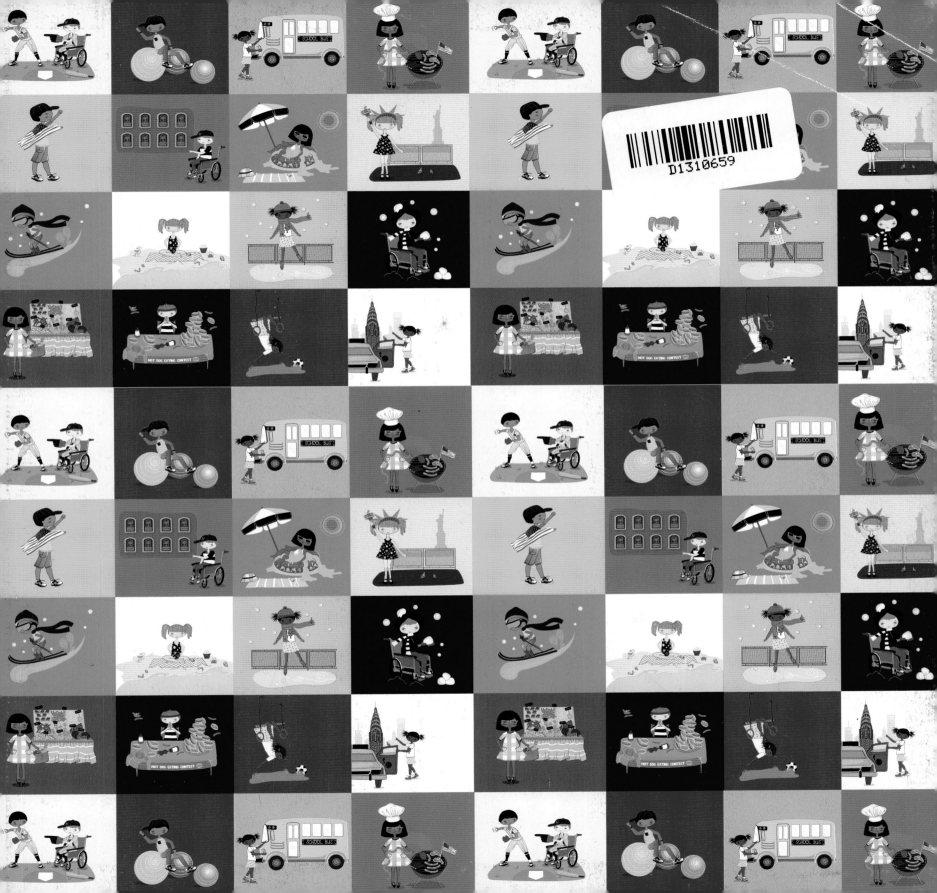

A New York YEAR

For Aussie New Yorkers, Jelena and Isis. With love. — TM

For everyone who has ever dreamed of New York. — TS

A New York YEAR

TWELVE MONTHS IN THE LIFE OF NEW YORK'S KIDS

TANIA MCCARTNEY + TINA SNERLING

Welcome to New York

Hola! My name is FABIAN and I'm 8. I was born in Puerto Rico and came to New York as a baby. I love football, and one day I want to be a wide receiver for the New York Giants.

Hi! I'm MADISON and I'm 10 years old. My grandparents came to New York from Ireland. I love ice-skating and Irish dancing, and one day I want to dance around the world.

Hey, my name is JAYLA. I'm 6 and I love drawing and painting with really bright colors. When I grow up, I want to be an artist. I also want to be a singer in a really cool band.

Buon giorno! I'm SOFIA. I'm 7 and I love animals. My family originally came from Italy. My nonna and I love to bake Italian treats, and one day I want to become a pastry chef.

Shalom. I'm ALEXANDER and my Jewish ancestors came from Germany a long time ago. I'm 9. I love reading and science, and when I grow up, I'd like to be an engineer.

JANUARY

It's NEW YEAR'S DAY! We have winter vacation.

January is our COLDEST month.
We have lots of snow!

POPCORN

REMOTE

CHIPS

BEAN BAG

BLANKET

We snuggle inside and watch MOVIES.

It's fun downloading
MUSIC to our iPods.

It's back to SCHOOL. We're
halfway through the school year.

HORSES

MONOPOLY

CHECKERS

DOLLS

Our FRIENDS come over to play.

We catch the bus, ride our bike or WALK to school.
In Manhattan, we catch the subway.

We have a SNOW DAY. No school!

EVERY
FOUR
YEARS

20TH

It's INAUGURATION Day.

The Children's
MUSEUM OF THE ARTS
in Manhattan is loads
of fun.

We lay FLOWERS at the 9/11 Memorial.

Martin Luther KING, Jr. Day

February

On Groundhog Day, we learn when SPRING will arrive.

2ND

IT'S GEORGE WASHINGTON'S BIRTHDAY!

PRESIDENT'S Day

We have SNOWBALL fights, and make snowmen and snow angels.

SOCCER

COPS AND ROBBERS

JUMPROPE

During recess and lunch, we love to get OUTDOORS.

The Empire State WINTER GAMES are held at Lake Placid.

 12TH

We CELEBRATE Lincoln's Birthday.

 14TH

On VALENTINE'S DAY, we give cards and candy and flowers.

15TH

SUSAN B. ANTHONY Day

CHIPS

POPCORN

CRACKERS

FRUIT

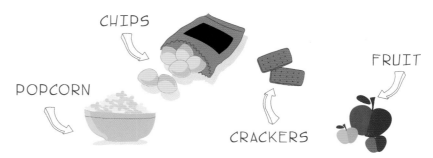

We love to gobble TREATS after school.

PASS THE CHALLAH!

On SHABBAT, we have a special meal together.

22ND

Fireworks pop during CHINESE NEW YEAR, which sometimes falls in January.

It's World Thinking Day for SCOUTS.

March

It's SPRING!

We have Spring BREAK.

2ND

On cold days, Mom makes HOT COCOA with marshmallows.

On Dr. Seuss's birthday, we celebrate BOOKS for Read Across America Day.

DAYLIGHT SAVING begins.
Clocks go forward one hour.

FLAGS wave outside the United Nations.

LET'S UNITE!

We keep busy after SCHOOL.

FOOTBALL TRAINING

DANCE

HOMEWORK

DANCE

We walk our DOGS in Central Park.

GREEN BEAR

SHAMROCKS

HORNS

GREEN HATS

17TH

The New York City ST. PATRICK'S DAY Parade is the biggest in the world!

Sometimes EASTER falls in March.

POTATOES

PINEAPPLE

WATERMELON

On the WEEKEND, we take a trip to our local farmers' market.

BROADWAY

Mom takes us to see a BROADWAY SHOW.

April

It's **APRIL FOOLS' DAY.** Dad freezes our cereal in the bowl!

1ST

It's **PASSOVER.** We host Seder at our house.

HAPPY PESACH!

THE YANKEES!

THE METS!

BASEBALL season begins!

On **ARBOR DAY**, we plant a new tree in our school yard.

We love **CANDY!**

JAWBREAKERS

GOBSTOPPERS

SUCKERS

LOLLIPOPS

PEANUT BUTTER CUPS

The DiMenna Children's History Museum makes **HISTORY COOL.**

On EASTER SUNDAY, we go to church and decorate eggs. We have egg hunts and an Easter parade.

TWOLEAF MITERWORT

VIOLET

WILD GINGER

WILD GERANIUM

WILDFLOWERS pop up all over the countryside.

LITTLE LEAGUE and softball seasons begin.

MAC AND CHEESE

TACOS

PORK AND RICE

PASTA

BURGERS

FLAVORED MILK

22ND

On EARTH DAY, we learn how to be green.

It's LUNCHTIME in the school cafeteria.

May

Cinco de Mayo is really COLORFUL! 5TH

It's WARMING up. We go to the local park to play.

It's MOTHER'S DAY. We just love our mom.

During FLEET WEEK, the Navy comes to town.

TEA

Happy Mother's Day!

FLOWERS

CHOCOLATES

The Children's Museum of Science and Technology has a really cool PLANETARIUM.

The view from the Empire State building is AMAZING!

AWESOME!

FISH WITH RICE

YUM!

SPAGHETTI

PIZZA

ICE CREAM

EMPANADAS

STEAK

LASAGNA

MAC AND CHEESE

We help make DINNER.

We ride the SUBWAY downtown.

Grandpa takes us to YANKEE Stadium.

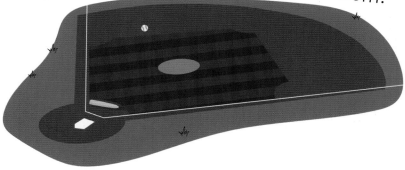

It's the Albany TULIP Festival.

On the weekend, we drive to Long Island and go SWIMMING at the beach.

On MEMORIAL DAY weekend, we have a BBQ with friends and family.

June

It's SUMMER!

It's CHILDREN'S DAY. We celebrate just being a kid.

14TH On FLAG DAY, the Stars and Stripes flies high.

WATCH OUT FOR POISON IVY!

Hiking *in the* HILLS is the best fun.

It's Summer VACATION. Almost three months off school!

SOCCER

BASEBALL

BASKETBALL

TENNIS

TEN-PIN BOWLING

We play so many SPORTS!

Dad takes us to the Baseball HALL OF FAME in Cooperstown.

On FATHER'S DAY, we celebrate our dad.

WORLD'S BEST DAD

We visit Howe Caverns in the CATSKILLS.

FLAVORED WATER

SODA

SHAKES

We love our DRINKS with tons of ice.

YUM YUM!

MANHATTAN has lots and lots of skyscrapers.

Magnolia Bakery CUPCAKES are delicious!

July

Macy's Fireworks Spectacular pops with some of the world's largest FIREWORKS!

4TH

The INDEPENDENCE DAY parade is awesome! We celebrate with family, friends, and fireworks.

WOW!

HOT DOG EATING CONTEST

CONEY ISLAND hosts the Fourth of July Hot Dog Eating Contest.

RAMADAN falls during different months of the year.

CHOCOLATE CHIP COOKIES

PIE

CUPCAKES

BROWNIES

We take over the kitchen and bake some TREATS.

Mom plants FLOWERS in the window boxes outside our apartment.

The torrone in Little Italy is SCRUMPTIOUS!

It's so much fun riding on the **STATEN ISLAND** Ferry.

It's so HOT, we drag out the kiddie pool.

Some of us go to SUMMER camps.

We visit the Metropolitan MUSEUM OF ART and the Guggenheim.

IT RUNS FOR OVER A MONTH!

It's HARLEM WEEK.

August

2ND

On FRIENDSHIP DAY, we celebrate our friends.

The Great New York State Fair is HUGE!

WHALES can be spied off the coast of New York.

ICE
LEMONS
SUGAR
PAPER CUPS

LEMONADE STAND $1

Everyone loves the LEMONADE stand on our block.

12TH

International YOUTH Day

WHAT A VIEW!

We climb the stairs, all the way to the Statue of Liberty's CROWN.

ROAD TRIP time! All the way to Niagara.

We eat POPSICLES to cool down.

We love a BAGEL with lox and
cream cheese from the local deli.

It's the Hong Kong Dragon Boat Festival in QUEENS.

Our family heads to Jones BEACH State Park.

27TH

Lyndon B. JOHNSON Day

The National Museum of Play in Rochester is super COOL.

September

Leaves start changing. It's FALL.

MARCO!

POLO!

It's LABOR DAY. We go swimming before it gets too cold!

The SCHOOL YEAR begins.

GRANDPARENTS' Day

Rosh Hashanah is the Jewish NEW YEAR.
We dip challah and apples in honey.
It can also fall in other months.

GO GIANTS!

GO JETS!

PARTY BAG

PASS THE PARCEL

DUCK DUCK GOOSE

MUSICAL CHAIRS

NFL season begins!

We celebrate our BIRTHDAYS with
cake and candles, presents, and games.

PATRIOT Day

11TH

CONSTITUTION Day

We the people

Bald eagles, osprey, and blue jays circle in the SKY above.

White is worn for YOM KIPPUR. Mom wears a prayer shawl to the synagogue. This holy day can also fall in other months.

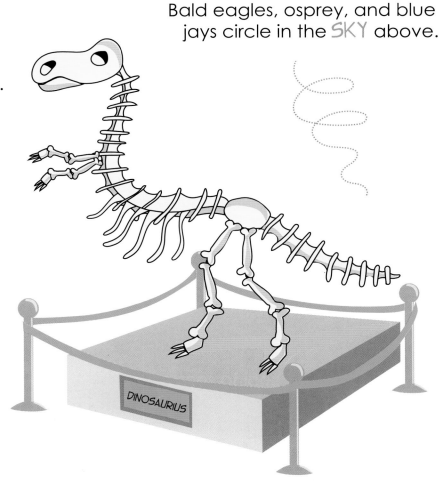

DINOSAURIUS

We learn a lot at the Children's Cultural Center of NATIVE America.

We go on a field trip to the NATURAL HISTORY Museum.

October

BROOKLYN NETS!

NEW YORK KNICKS!

It's World TEACHERS' Day.

5TH

COLUMBUS Day

We choose the fattest Jack-O'-Lantern PUMPKIN at our local pumpkin patch.

GERMAN-American Day

It's OKTOBERFEST.

6TH

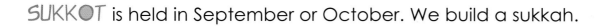

SUKKOT is held in September or October. We build a sukkah.

Abuela makes the best CHURROS ever.

RICO!

We rake LEAVES into piles ... and jump!

Travel back to when the PLANET began
at Museum of the Earth in Ithaca.

Mom and Dad love JAZZ.

YELLOW BIRCH

SUGAR MAPLE

AMERICAN BEECH

RED MAPLE

COBWEBS

WITCHES

TOMBSTONES

JACK-O'-LANTERN

R.I.P.

31ST

PUMPKINS

The Adirondacks are ABLAZE
with leaves in orange, red, and gold.

It's HALLOWEEN. Time for some trick-or-treating!

November

DAYLIGHT SAVING ends.

CLOCKS GO BACK

THANK YOU!

11TH

We remember our servicemen and women on **VETERANS DAY**.

BREAKFAST is delicious at our house.

PANCAKES

EGGS

OATMEAL

BAGELS

WAFFLES

HOWL!

Bobcats, gray wolves, black bears, and cougars stalk our **STATE** parks.

The days are getting **SHORTER**.

SNOW starts fluttering down. We polish up our skis!

We run with Dad in the New York City **MARATHON**.

America **RECYCLES** Day

15TH

20TH   It's Universal *CHILDREN'S* Day.

On THANKSGIVING, we feast with friends and family … and give thanks.

PUMPKIN PIE

POTATOES

CRANBERRY SAUCE

GREEN BEAN CASSEROLE

TURKEY

We love the Macy's Thanksgiving Day PARADE.

LIGHTS

The Rockefeller Center CHRISTMAS TREE has 30,000 lights!

December

WINTER creeps in.

15 Opera House Rd,
Sydney, NSW
2000

We send Christmas **GREETING CARDS** to friends and family far away.

It's Christmas **VACATION**!

We love to go **CAROLING** in our neighborhood.

Mom makes a different **ADVENT** calendar every year.

VERY IMPORTANT DAY

10

It's **HUMAN RIGHTS** Day.

It's **HANUKKAH**. We light our Hanukiah.

WREATH

CANDY CANES

MISTLETOE

POPCORN STRINGS

LIGHTS

Dad hangs the **MISTLETOE** and we decorate the tree.

During KWANZAA, we celebrate family, community, and culture.

HABARI GANI!

On CHRISTMAS EVE, we hang stockings and listen for Santa Claus!

24TH

EGGNOG

ROAST PORK

APPLE PIE

DUCK

GREEN BEAN CASSEROLE

ROAST HAM   STUFFING   COOKIES   MASHED POTATOES

25TH On CHRISTMAS DAY, we go to church then come home to a luscious feast.

HAPPY NEW YEAR!

It's FESTIVUS!

31ST On NEW YEAR'S EVE, the big ball drops at Times Square. We welcome an awesome new year.

Our State

STATE FACTS

NICKNAME: Empire State
SONG: *I Love New York*
FLOWER: Rose
TREE: Sugar Maple
PLANT: Lilac Bush
MOTTO: Excelsior
FRUIT: Apple
SNACK: Yogurt
GEM: Garnet
BIRD: Eastern Bluebird
MAMMAL: Beaver
FISH: Brook Trout
INSECT: Nine-Spotted Ladybug
SHELL: Bay Scallop

NEW YORK WAS NAMED AFTER ENGLAND'S DUKE OF YORK.

THERE ARE 62 COUNTIES IN NEW YORK.

NEW YORK STATE IS HOME TO 58 SPECIES OF WILD ORCHID.

LAKE ERIE

The Adirondack region hosts the largest protected natural area in the lower 48 states.

New York is amazing!

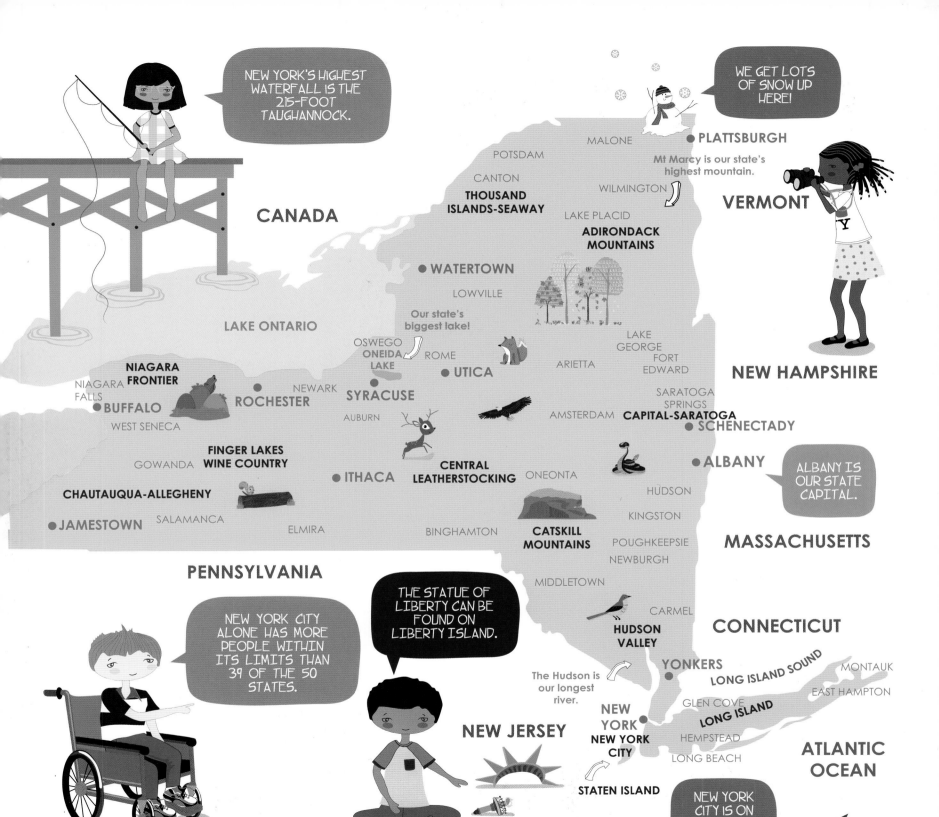

A huge thank you to New York advisors Devon Sillett and Yitka Winn, and to the kids of Ethical Community Charter School in Jersey City and P.S./I.S. 210 Twenty-First Century Academy For Community Leadership in Manhattan. Unending thanks to Anouska Jones and the team at Exisle for their support. — TM + TS

First published 2016

EK Books
an imprint of Exisle Publishing Pty Ltd
'Moonrising', Narone Creek Road,
Wollombi, NSW 2325, Australia
P.O. Box 60-490, Titirangi
Auckland 0642, New Zealand
www.ekbooks.com.au

A CiP record for this book is available from the National Library of Australia

ISBN 978 1 925335 07 1

Designed and typeset by Tina Snerling.
Typeset in Century Gothic, Street Cred and custom fonts
Printed in China
This book uses paper sourced under ISO 1 4001 guidelines from well-managed forests and other controlled sources.

10 9 8 7 6 5 4 3 2 1

Author Note

This is by no means a comprehensive listing of the events and traditions celebrated by New York's multitude of ethnic people. The entries in this book have been chosen to reflect a range of modern lifestyles for the majority of New York's children, with a focus on traditional endemic elements and themes, which are in themselves a glorious mishmash of present, past, introduced and endemic culture. Content in this book has been produced in consultation with native New York advisors, school teachers, and school children, with every intention of respecting the cultural and idiosyncratic elements of New York and its people.